FIRST EXPERIENCES

FERN'S FIRST TIME AT THE FARM

by Katie Chanez
illustrated by Daniela Massironi

GRASSHOPPER

Tools for Parents & Teachers

Grasshopper Books enhance imagination and introduce the earliest readers to fiction with fun storylines and illustrations. The easy-to-read text supports early reading experiences with repetitive sentence patterns and sight words.

Before Reading

- Look at the cover illustration. What do readers see? What do they think the book will be about?
- Look at the picture glossary together. Sound out the words. Ask readers to identify the first letter of each vocabulary word.

During Reading

- "Walk" through the book with the reader. Discuss new or unfamiliar words. Sound them out together.
- Look at the pictures together. Point out any labels.

After Reading

- Review the picture glossary again. Ask readers to locate the words in the text.
- Ask the reader: How did Fern feel while meeting the animals? How do you know?

Grasshopper Books are published by Jump!
3500 American Blvd W, Suite 150
Bloomington, MN 55431
www.jumplibrary.com

Jump! is a division of FlutterBee Education Group.

Library of Congress Cataloging-in-Publication Data

Names: Chanez, Katie, author.
Massironi, Daniela, illustrator.
Title: Fern's first time at the farm / by Katie Chanez;
illustrated by Daniela Massironi.
Description: Minneapolis, MN: Jump!, Inc., 2026.
Series: First experiences
Audience: Ages 3–6.
Identifiers: LCCN 2024044522 (print)
LCCN 2024044523 (ebook)
ISBN 9798892138734 (hardcover)
ISBN 9798892138741 (paperback)
ISBN 9798892138758 (ebook)
Subjects: CYAC: Emotions—Fiction. | Farms—Fiction.
LCGFT: Picture books.
Classification: LCC PZ7.1.C4794 Fe 2026 (print)
LCC PZ7.1.C4794 (ebook)
DDC [E] —dc23
LC record available at https://lccn.loc.gov/2024044522
LC ebook record available at https://lccn.loc.gov/2024044523

Editor: Alyssa Sorenson
Direction and Layout: Molly Ballanger
Illustrator: Daniela Massironi

Printed in the United States of America at
Corporate Graphics in North Mankato, Minnesota.

Table of Contents

New Sights and Smells

We are going to a farm.

It is my first time.

Farmer Lacy waves to us.

The cows moo.

They are loud.

We go in the barn.

"Ew!" I say. "It smells."

"Do you want to pet the pigs, Fern?" asks Farmer Lacy.

I shake my head.

We go outside.

Horses gallop.

“Wow, they are fast!” I say.

“Come feed the goats,” says Dad.

“They are cute,” I say.

One jumps up.

It scares me.

"It is OK," says Farmer Lacy.
"He is just excited."

She helps me feed the goat.

It tickles.

I like the farm!

Let's Review!

Fern does not like the farm at first. How do we know?

A. She runs away from the horses.
B. She covers her ears.
C. She does not pet the pigs.
D. She feeds the goats.

Picture Glossary

barn
A large farm building in which animals, crops, or equipment are kept.

cute
Charming and pretty.

gallop
To run fast with all four feet off the ground at once.

tickles
Touches or pokes gently in a way that makes someone laugh.

Let's Review! Answer Key: **B.** She covers her ears. **C.** She does not pet the pigs.